To my daughters, Zoe and Riley, who asked the question that inspired this book.
I pray that each of you will see yourselves the way God sees you.
You are so special to me.

To my husband, David--thank you for helping me finish this project,
and for being the best person I know.

To my parents, Tim and Robin, who taught me these messages from
an early age and have never stopped learning and growing--thank you.
Thank you to each of my brothers and sisters for being you
--a necessary part of our family.

And a special dedication to my grandparents--
Ralph, who taught me to keep having fun even when childhood ends.
Jean, who was everyone's friend. George, who encouraged me to dream big.
Luella, who taught me to dream with God.
Thank you for being my partner in this project and for using your gifts
to bring Maya and this story to life.

First edition published 2021

ISBN: 9798504393001

To request permissions, contact the author at
sarahbonnema@gmail.com.

Book layout by Charity Russell
www.charityrussell.com

The COLOR of GOD

Written by
Sarah
Morgenthaler Bonnema

Illustrated by
Luella Morgenthaler

Maya and Mama were coloring one day,
when Maya asked, "Mama, what color is God?"

Mama's face lit up. She leaned forward.
And she smiled.
"Now, THAT is a good question," she said.
"Let's find out!"

"What color is the sky?" Mama asked.
"Blue," Maya said.
"Yes," Mama said. "Today, it looks blue. But…"

"What color is the sky on a rainy day,
when we're wearing our boots and splashing
in puddles and feeling cold drops on our skin?"
"Gray," Maya said.

"And what color is the sky when Mama's making coffee
and you're eating toast and we're sitting in soft pajamas,
reading at the breakfast table, loving one another?"
"Pink and red and orange-y yellow!" Maya said.

"And what color is the sky when we're saying goodnight
to Beary and Kitty and Mr. Turtle and Scruffy the Owl
—when we're saying prayers and turning off the lights
and drinking our last time water?"
"Well," Maya thought, "Black! And white with stars.
And gray with city lights…"

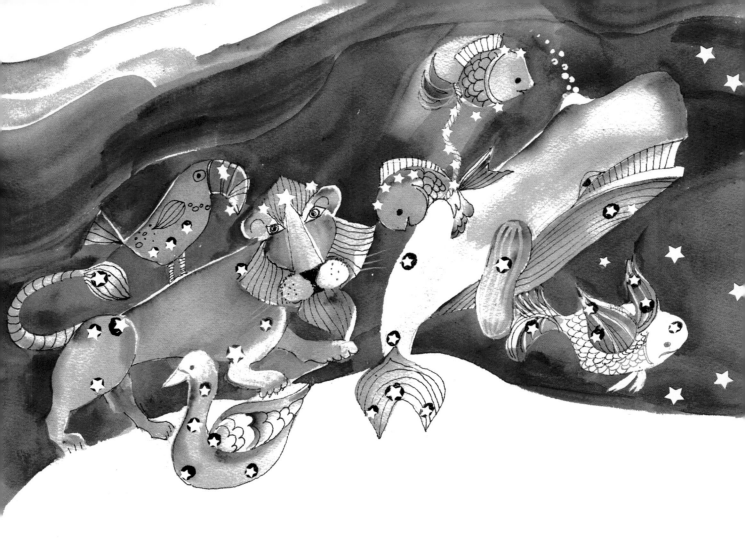

"And what color are those stars, really?"
Mama asked.
"The ones up there in the sky, in shapes that tell stories?"
"My teacher said some stars are blue,"
Maya said.

"Yes. And some are red, and some are gold,"
Mama said.
"And the planets up there are gray and blue
and orange and yellow and white!"
"That's a lot of colors!" Maya said.

"And that's just the sky!" Mama said. "We haven't talked about what's beneath our feet! What color is the ground outside?"

"Green," said Maya, thinking of the park.

"Unless we're at the beach," Mama said. "Then it's—"
"White!" Maya said. "Like flour when we make pancakes!"

"And what about the duck pond?"
Mama asked.
"What colors do you see when we look down and feed the ducks?"
"Green grass," Maya said.
"Brown mud. And water that reflects the sky
—and trees—and me!"

"And what color are those ducks, gliding through the water,
coming for your bread crumbs?"
Mama asked.
"Green. And brown! And orange on their funny feet,"
giggled Maya.

"But are all birds green and brown?" asked Mama.
Maya thought—about cardinals and blue jays
and the seeds they ate—
about flamingos and toucans
and parrots and
peacocks and eagles
and vultures

and those tiny little
yellow-bellied birds
that said
"Chick-a-dee-dee-dee…"

"No," Maya said.
"Birds are ALL colors!
I learned THAT from my bird book."

"And their eggs are different colors, too," Mama continued.
"Remember when we found that nest last week?"
Maya smiled, thinking of tree climbing and nest finding
and egg staring and bird guessing.

"Mama?" Maya asked.
"Do you think God knows what the birds inside the
eggs are going to look like before they hatch?"
"Yes," Mama said. "Because God made them."

Maya thought about that for a minute.

"Does God know what everything is going to look like before it's here?"

Mama smiled, and answered,

"Yes, because God makes everything—
and God makes everything wonderful!"

Then Maya asked:
"Did God make the zebra black and white?"

"And the pig, pink and curly tailed?"

"And the trees—tall and green, and then,
in the fall, red and yellow and brown?"

"And the flowers—oh, the flowers!
Every color? Really?"
Mama just kept nodding.

"The red apples? And the green ones?
And the yellow ones?"
"Yes, yes, and yes," Mama said, continuing:

"God made Gracie the puppy soft brown,
and Snips the cat white and fluffy,
and Olivia the fish with rainbow scales.
God made ME with peach skin
and YOU with chocolate skin
and EVERYONE with their hair
and eyes and mouth and hands to share love."

Mama asked: "Maya, when you paint, when you draw,
when you use clay—do you like to use one color,
or do you like to use them all?"

"I like to use them all!" Maya said.

Mama smiled and said, "God is the same way."

"And so, my sweet Maya--
God isn't a color.
God is the source of ALL the colors.
And they're ALL God's favorite."

"And so, if you want to know what color God is--
Look around the world at all God created.

And enjoy."

Made in the USA
Middletown, DE
09 July 2021